Praise for *Off to the Races with Mukha the Dingo*

"Ray Chung has written a delightful children's story based upon a beloved local event as seen through the eyes of Mukha, a dingo. The illustrations by Emily Hurst Pritchett depict the charm and allure of hunt racing during the autumn season in Virginia and will captivate both children and adults. A must-read."

—Trish Crowe, founder of the Firnew Farm Artists' Circle, author of *Madison County (Images of America, Virginia)*, and board member of the Montpelier Foundation.

· ·

"Say hello to funny and energetic Mukha the dingo! When Mukha unexpectedly finds herself all alone in the midst of a horse racing event, she must rely on her courage and wits to locate her humans. As Mukha scurries through the large and noisy crowd of strangers, she refuses to allow difficult challenges or fear discourage her. Mukha shows us that even when a situation seems hopeless, love finds a way to turn the unexpected into something adventurous and wonderful!"

—Pamela Adler, author of *Maddy and Mia: TriPaw Tales*

· ·

"A delightful, feel-good tale with perfectly brilliant illustrations. Put me down as a big Mukha fan."

—Martin Clark, bestselling author of *The Substitution Order*

· ·

"*Off to the Races with Mukha the Dingo* features gorgeous illustrations and a fabulous, spirited story filled with heart. Readers young and old will fall in love with Mukha—who's based on an amazing real-life Carolina Dog/American Dingo—while learning a bit about the beautiful Virginian countryside, as well as some invaluable life lessons. Highly recommended for kids aged 1–100+."

—Greg Levin, award-winning author of books for kids aged 18–100+

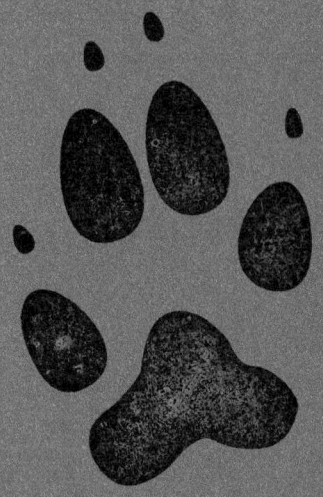

Best wishes,
Rony Clung

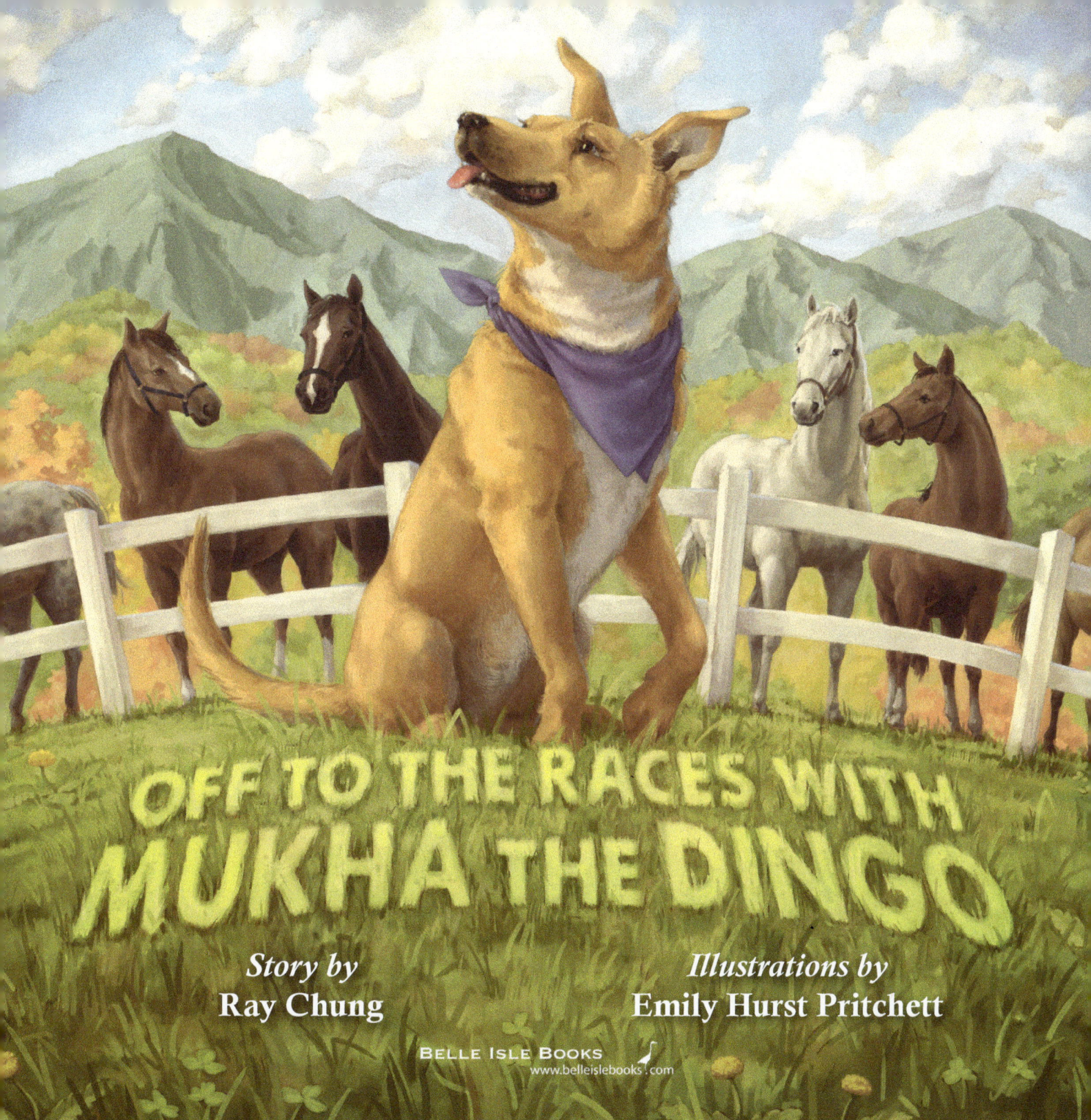

This book in no way endorses bringing pets to horse racing events.

Copyright © 2022 by Raymond K. Chung, MD

No part of this book may be reproduced in any form or by any electronic or mechanical means, or the facilitation thereof, including information storage and retrieval systems, without permission in writing from the publisher, except in the case of brief quotations published in articles and reviews. Any educational institution wishing to photocopy part or all of the work for classroom use, or individual researchers who would like to obtain permission to reprint the work for educational purposes, should contact the publisher.

ISBN: 9781953021304
LCCN: 2021921057

Designed by Michael Hardison
Project managed by Grace Ball

Printed in the United States of America

Published by
Belle Isle Books (an imprint of Brandylane Publishers, Inc.)
5 S. 1st Street
Richmond, Virginia 23219

BELLE ISLE BOOKS
www.belleislebooks.com

belleislebooks.com | brandylanepublishers.com

To my mom, Vicky, and dad, Shih-Yung,
who have supported me throughout the years,
both financially and emotionally, and to whom I owe everything.
Without them, none of this would have been possible (literally!).

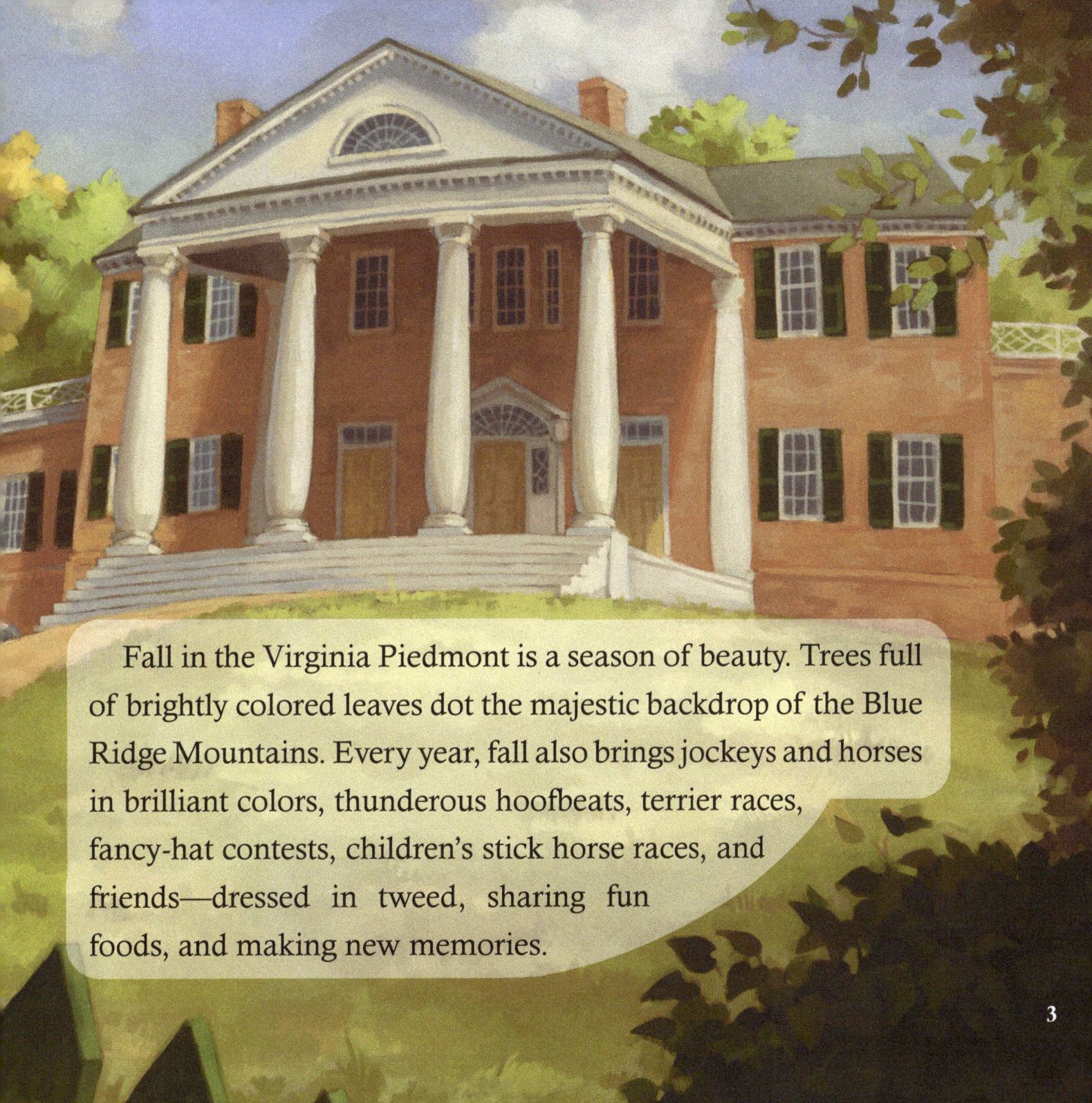

Fall in the Virginia Piedmont is a season of beauty. Trees full of brightly colored leaves dot the majestic backdrop of the Blue Ridge Mountains. Every year, fall also brings jockeys and horses in brilliant colors, thunderous hoofbeats, terrier races, fancy-hat contests, children's stick horse races, and friends—dressed in tweed, sharing fun foods, and making new memories.

Naturally shy, but incredibly curious, Mukha climbed into the back of her humans' pickup truck.

Why is there so much stuff in the truck today? she wondered. Mukha looked around at the big coolers, folded tables, and stacks of chairs.

Where could the humans be going?

Mukha peeked over the edge of the truck. *Uh-oh . . . maybe climbing into the back of the truck wasn't such a good idea.* The truck had started moving! Mukha was going farther and farther away from home!

After what felt like a long time, the truck started to slow. The road became windier and bumpier, and Mukha began hearing strange human voices.

Where are we? Mukha wondered as she looked out from the back of the truck. *Look at all these nicely dressed people!* Mukha saw ladies in lovely hats and men wearing tweed jackets. *Everyone seems to be having so much fun,* thought Mukha, and she stepped up onto the edge of the truck to get a better look. *What wonderful smells. I bet those treats are tasty, too—*

All of a sudden, the truck hit a bump, and Mukha bounced right out! She landed on a soft pile of leaves. Mukha popped up, ready to run after her humans' truck, when a big sign hanging on a fence stopped her in her tracks. On the sign was a picture of a dog. The dog had a red circle around it, with a slash running through.

"No dogs allowed," Mukha whispered. She thought about what might happen if she got caught.

Will I get kicked out before I find my humans? Will I go to dog jail?!

Mukha took a deep, calming breath. *All I have to do is find my humans, and they'll take me home,* thought Mukha. She looked around for her humans' truck, but there were so many people and tall tents and tables, she couldn't see the truck or her humans anywhere. *How am I ever going to find them?* Mukha wondered.

Feeling lost and scared, Mukha quickly looked for a place to hide. She saw a pack of terriers chasing a brightly colored toy along a course lined with hay bales. *Maybe they can help me find my humans!* thought Mukha.

Mukha jumped over a hay bale and caught up with the terriers. "Hello! Have you seen my humans?" Mukha asked them.

But the terriers continued running—not one even looked over at Mukha! Their eyes were trained on the colorful toy in front of them, just out of reach.

Mukha tried once more. "Please! Have you seen my humans?!" she asked breathlessly; but it was no use. Frustrated, Mukha gave up and ran ahead of them, toward a row of well-decorated tables. *The terriers weren't helpful,* thought Mukha. *From now on, I've got to stay out of sight while I try to find my humans.*

Overhead, Mukha heard an announcer report, "Attention, everyone. The winner of the terrier race finals is . . . a dingo? Was that a dingo?"

As Mukha sneaked between tailgates, she spotted a man trying to carry an armful of supplies while dragging a large cooler behind him. *He sure looks like he could use some help,* Mukha thought; and she ran over to grab the other end of the cooler.

Once Mukha and the man reached his tailgate, they set the cooler down. The man turned to offer thanks just in time to catch a glimpse of Mukha darting off.

As she ran away, Mukha heard the man say, "I think that was a dingo!"

Mukha ran until she found another row of tables to hide under. *I can't find my humans anywhere!*

Mukha peeked over the table she was hiding under and saw a stuffed toy fox looking out over the crowd. *The view might be better from up there!*

Mukha hopped onto the table and stood motionless next to the toy fox, looking out as hard and far as she could. Mukha didn't see her humans, but she did see tables and tables full of yummy treats!

Look at all this food! thought Mukha. When no one was looking, Mukha darted over to a table to help herself to some of the tastiest-looking treats. *I'm going to try one of these . . . and maybe one of those . . . and definitely this one!*

Just as Mukha was about to get a treat, she saw one of the trays sliding off the edge of the table. Mukha ran over just in time to catch the tray on the top of her head and nudge it back onto the table. Mukha heard a human close by say, "Thanks for saving our tray of food!"

Mukha had been spotted! She dashed off. Behind her, she heard people say, "Was that a dingo?!"

Mukha ran under tables and slipped between tents—but before she knew what had happened, there were flowers, bows, and ribbons piled on top of her head. Mukha was covered in tailgate decorations! As she ran, a ribbon fell in front of her eyes, and Mukha couldn't see a thing!

Finally, Mukha made it to a quiet spot. She pawed at the ribbon covering her eyes. *How am I going to get all this stuff off my head?* she wondered.

Mukha continued to paw at the ribbon until finally, she could see again. Right away, Mukha saw a crowd gathered around and a row of ladies standing alongside her. *They're wearing fancy decorations on their heads, too!*

One of the ladies looked down at Mukha and chuckled. Worried that her luck had run out and she'd finally been caught, Mukha took off running again. The sound of her paws on the ground was drowned out by the announcer saying, "What? How is that possible? A dingo has won the ladies hat contest!"

Looking for cover, Mukha ran until she arrived at a row of bushes. *A wonderful place to hide,* thought Mukha. As she wiggled in between two bushes, the branches pulled the tailgate decorations off her head.

Happy as she was to have gotten rid of the decorations, Mukha couldn't leave the tangled mess stuck in the branches. *Now, where should I put all this?* she wondered.

Mukha picked up the pile, making sure to get every little piece. She looked around and spotted a garbage can not far from her. As she placed the pile into the bin, Mukha saw a group of children looking at her. *Yikes!*

"Was that a dingo?" Mukha heard one of the little girls ask her friends.

Mukha ran alongside the row of bushes until she came upon a big group of horses. The horses were wearing fancy colors, and there were humans near them, wearing fancy colors to match!

The terriers weren't able to help, thought Mukha, *but the horses are so tall—they might have seen my humans somewhere in the crowd.*

Mukha sneaked over to one of the horses and asked, "Hello up there! Have you seen my humans?"

The horse looked down at Mukha. "Oh, hello! You happened along at the right time. The race is about to begin! If you've lost someone, you should come with us. You will have a much better view from inside the course, and you may be able to spot your humans from there."

"Thank you so much! That's a great idea!" replied Mukha.

Mukha followed as the horses lined up to start the race. Suddenly, there was a loud *bang*! Mukha was so startled that she ran. She ran so fast that it wasn't long before she was ahead of all the horses!

As she ran, Mukha heard the announcer's voice over the speaker, "They're off! And the early lead goes to . . . a little tan horse without a jockey . . ."

Mukha kept running, searching the crowd as she went.

The announcer continued, "And they're over the first jump! Still in the lead is the little tan horse without a jockey . . . and without a number?"

Wow, the view really is better out here on the course! thought Mukha. As she and the horses cleared the second jump and rounded the third turn, Mukha spotted familiar faces in the crowd. *There they are! My humans!*

Overhead, the announcer said, "Wait, that's not a little tan horse. Is that a dingo?"

At the same time, Mukha's humans saw her leading the race—and heading directly toward them!

Mukha jumped over the fence and into the outstretched arms of her humans.

"Mukha! What are you doing here?" her mom asked.

Mukha jumped and wiggled with excitement. She was so relieved to finally be back with her family!

As Mukha and her humans celebrated being back together, a group of people approached. Mukha saw two race officials among them and hid behind her humans.

"Is that your dingo?" one official asked.

Uh-oh, this is it! I'm going to dog jail, thought Mukha.

"Why, yes, she is," replied Mukha's dad. "Are we in trouble?"

"Well," said the official, "as I'm sure you know, we don't allow dogs other than those in the terrier competition here at the Virginia Hunt Classic." The official looked down at Mukha, and she huddled closer to her mom's leg.

The race official continued. "However, your dingo won the terrier race finals, and she also won the ladies hat contest," she said, smiling as she handed two first-place ribbons to Mukha's humans.

Surprised, Mukha peeked at the officials from behind her mom.

"We also have it on good authority that your dingo was quite helpful to attendees throughout the day, and she set a good example for these children." The official gestured to the children who had seen Mukha place the tailgate decorations in the garbage can.

The official crouched in front of Mukha. "Therefore, we'd all like her to stay," she said as he reached out to pet her.

Mukha beamed as she stepped forward to accept all her belly rubs and ribbons!

What an incredible day at the races!

Our beloved Mukha crossed the Rainbow Bridge unexpectedly before her book was published. Sharing her story with you helps keep her memory alive. We hope this book gives you some idea of the great joy she brought to our family. To Mukha the Dingo, gone too soon.

Acknowledgments

Thanks to the canids around the world and especially to those who were kind enough to share their journey on the earth with us humans. Dogs are truly "man's best friend."

To Scooter, Ginger, Cala, and Mukha, who have gone on before. Thanks to Bentley, Jesse, and Ferdinand, who continue to inspire me. This is their legacy.

Thanks to my family, friends, and Barbie, who have put up with me through the years.

Thanks to my publishing team for believing in the project and for guiding this novice, and to my illustrator, Emily, whose splendid illustrations have made this an updated classic.

Finally, to the readers now and in the future who will be experiencing a Virginia tradition and will be helping to keep Mukha's memory alive.

About the Author

Ray Chung is a graduate of the University of Pennsylvania and Jefferson Medical College. He is a practicing orthopedic hand surgeon, who is blessed to live in the Virginia Piedmont with his rescue pups. Ray wishes to share their antics and a glimpse of country life to entertain and enlighten kids around the world. He helps maintain Mukha's Instagram page @mukhathedingo in her memory.

About the Illustrator

Emily grew up in western New York and has loved to draw and paint all her life. She studied illustration at Brigham Young University in Utah before moving back to the East Coast. She loves to read books for kids and grown-ups, sing, dance, and play video games. She currently lives in Boston, where she loves to hike in the woods with her husband and son. You can find more about Emily at her website, emilypritchettart.com.

Printed in the USA
CPSIA information can be obtained
at www.ICGtesting.com
LVHW060631280324
775709LV00010B/73